Taking Care of Yourself Is Important

by Ms. Merriweather's class
with Tony Stead

capstone® classroom

We think it's important to take care of yourself.

Hooray for staying clean!

Washing your hands stops you from getting bad germs.

Brushing your teeth stops smelly breath.

Brushing your hair gets rid of tangles and makes you look neat.

Washing your face takes dirt and oil off your skin.

Taking a bath makes you smell clean and fresh.

We always remember to take care of ourselves. You should too!

What do you do to take care of yourself?